HER FAVOURITE LITTLE SEX TOY

"a female domination, male submission bisexual erotica"

By Daniel P. Elliot

CONTENTS

IT'S TIME FOR SOME CHANGES...

"Darling, how would like to meet up at that cafe you like this lunchtime for something to eat?"

"Oh Charles, that's a wonderful idea,"

"12 o'clock a good time for you?"

"Yes, and we'll meet outside the sex shop that's just around the corner from the cafe, if that's okay with you."

"You want to meet outside the sex shop?"

"Yes, that's right - outside the sex shop, and after we've done a bit if shopping you can treat me to lunch," Eleanor smiled, as she lathered the soap into her husband's cock and balls.

"I don't understand... why do you want to meet there?" Charles asked.

"Well... I was thinking that it would be a good idea to buy some porn movies to watch while we enjoy a few glasses of wine together this evening," she said as she slowly moved her hand between his buttocks and toward his arse hole, "and I was also thinking that we could try something a little different tonight... something adventurous." she continued, pushing the tip of her middle finger into her husband's tight arse, making him gasp and his cock start to harden.

The pleasurable feeling of his wife's index finger moving in and out of his arse hole made Charles groan. She looked down at his erect cock and smiled. "It looks like I've already found something different that you seem to enjoy," she teased.

"Fuck yes..." Charles moaned, "It feels good,"

Eleanor crouched down in front of her husband and took his cock into her open mouth while pushing her finger deeper into his tight arse. He let out another low groan as she sucked his throbbing cock in her mouth and teased his arse, knowing that he would soon cum as deep inside this small act of long forgotten curiosity of anal pleasure had added a new dimension to the couple's sex life – but suddenly Eleanor stopped what she was doing and climbed out of the shower.

She grabbed the bath towel from the rail and wrapped it around her hour-glass figure. '"If we get the porn's this lunchtime, then we'll continue tonight." she smiled, closing the bathroom door behind her, "oh, and do me a favour - stay in the shower until I've gone to work, that's a good boy!"

Needless to say, Charles was somewhat distracted in the office that morning while his mind kept wandering back and forth to the scene in the shower and what his wife had said to him. He had noticed how his beautiful wife had become increasingly horny over the past weeks, but he had put that purely down to spending a second honeymoon in Barcelona to put the spark back into their relationship, after a slightly rocky patch in their marriage. But he couldn't have been further from the truth and had no idea of the real reason behind his wife's increasing sexual appetite.

Charles glanced at his gold wristwatch and after what seemed like an eternity - it was finally lunchtime. He could feel how wet the front of his boxer shorts had become over the last couple of hours and checked to see if his throbbing dick and possible damp patch were not too noticeable, but with his mind focused on what they were about to do, it was very evident that he was sexually excited. He did what he could only do and draped his coat over his arm in front of his chest and began walking toward the lift.

***

Ten minutes later Charles arrived outside the sex shop, relieved to see Eleanor already there waiting.

She greeted him with a loving kiss. "Are you ready to go inside?" She asked, taking him by the arm and literally dragging him through the blackened door. They made their way straight toward the porn movies, passing the large array of dildos, vibrators and other contraptions that were on display along the way.

"Do you see anything you like?" She asked as they stopped at the dildo display.

"What?" Charles replied slightly surprised.

"Which one would you like to see sliding in and out of my pussy tonight?"

Charles could hardly believe that his wife had just said what she had, and looked around to see if anyone had heard her.

"Charles, for God's sake... we're in a bleedin' sex shop, people in here are only here for one thing...SEX!" she laughed, enjoying every moment of her husband's embarrassment.

"Okay, let's try and make this easier for you. Do you like this one?' She said, reaching for a big flesh coloured dildo with a suction cup at the base and placed it in his hand.

"Er...fine," he replied, trying to shake off the embarrassment of being embarrassed.

"Mmm... It feels good, looks good, and we can use it together in the shower," She said, taking it from her husband and stroking it in her petite hand, "That was a very good choice, Darling... now let's go and choose some naughty movies, shall we?"

They began looking through the wide range of movies and it did not take long for them to choose a couple of DVDs. Eleanor had chosen a couple of bondage movies involving leather clad woman dominating their male partners, while Charles opted for a selection of threesome pornos.

"This should do," Eleanor said as she picked up a very large tub of lubrication for her new sex toy before proceeding to the young gentleman standing behind the counter. Is there anything else you are interested in, Darling?" she asked looking towards the male underwear, "Oh, I'd love to see you in a pair of tight latex undies."

"Sure," Charles replied, knowing damn well that his wife knew exactly what would interest him, (The couple had often talked about latex and rubber wear, but had never got round to buying any – until now) "I think you should buy something latex as well for yourself," he suggested.

Eleanor decided on a shiny soft black PVC thong, open crotch latex panties, suspender belt and stockings and Charles came back with a choice of latex underpants. "Which ones do you like?" he asked, showing her what he had found.

"I like the red Hipster style ones as these will really show off that sexy arse of yours, but there's something missing," she answered, "Here, hold these for a second." she said handing him the garments before walking over to where Charles had found the Hipsters.

She returned with a naughty look on her face. "You should take these as well," she smiled while holding up a pair of latex shorts with a penis sheath. "Not only will your arse look hot in them, but I'll get nine inches of black cock deep inside me tonight."

One look at them and Charles knew he could not wait to try them on, the thought of tight latex around his cock and balls began to turn him on. They paid the young gentleman for the goods and left the shop.

Eleanor handed Charles the latex underwear. "Here, take these. I want you to go back to the office and spend the rest of the day wearing them, and I also want you to stroke your latex cock throughout the afternoon and fill it with as much pre-cum as possible without actually ejaculating – don't forget," she said with a stern look on her face, "I want your cock and balls covered in as much pre-cum as possible when you return home this evening and then we continue from where we left off in the shower."

With that, she left. Now Charles was fully erect and he could feel his cock already leaking valuable spunk, which was soaking into my shorts. He rushed back to the office to change as fast as he could.

This day was definitely the day when Charles began to realise that his wife was starting to become more dominant and taking control of their sex life, but he had not yet comprehended where her dominance would soon lead them.

WILL YOU TAKE THE
RED PILL?

Waiting to meet Eleanor for lunch had been painful enough, but having to wait until he finished in the office at five o'clock was almost unbearable. The short journey home was just a blur, as he pictured the scenarios of what lay ahead for him later that evening - over and over in his mind.

Soon he was home and pinned on the back door was a note, Charles xx wrote in his wife's handwriting. It read:

Dearest Charles,

Don't bother trying to get into the house as I have locked the door from the inside. This evening is all about me and my desires; you will be used to pleasure my desire and only mine. If you achieve this then I will give you the sexual release you will be certainly requiring.

But first there are a few rules you must obey tonight:

Rule No.1 - no talking unless I begin the conversation!

Rule No.2 - you will not ejaculate until I'm sexually satisfied or I command you to do so!

Rule No.3 - We will NOT discuss any of my planned events tonight until I initiate the conversation. This also includes if you decide not to go through with tonight!

Breaking any of these rules will result in consequences and you will pay for this in a manner I deem suitable for the disobedience.

Now you have to make the decision to either let me dominate our sexual journeys from now on or return to our happy and content bedroom routines. But before you make this decision remember that I love you and always have, even during the rough times and I will always respect your decision. You have liberated me from my sexual inhibitions and for that I am grateful. Now I would like to free you from yours in return but in the ways of my choosing.

Decision time my darling, will you take the blue pill and decide 'no' and take the spare key from under the plant pot and enter the house, sorry I lied about locking the door! Or will you take the 'red pill' and follow Alice down the rabbit hole by reading my next note that's hidden under the plant pot with the key?

Door key or note Charles?

Your loving wife

Eleanor xxx

P.S. Either way, I AM going to ride that latex cock of yours tonight!

Charles just stood there open-mouthed, with his stubble chin to the floor. His cock was harder than ever with even more pre-cum flowing around the latex pants. The words in the letter had grabbed his attention, raised his curiosity and overloaded his filthy imagination by their suggestive connotations. *'Liberate me from my sexual inhibitions'*, *'free you from yours'*, *'I command you and ride that latex cock'*. There are moments in life when reality stops you dead in your tracks, excites or numbs your senses to comprehend what is playing out in front of you. Needless to say that this was one of those heart-stopping moments and Charles was enslaved in sexual arousal.

Without even noticing it, he had already begun rubbing the impressive bulge in his trousers. He could feel the veins of his cock protruding under the thin membrane of the underpants and the ripple of foreskin tightly pulled back to reveal the swollen head of his well-lubricated member. An afternoon of pooled cum began washing over his scooter and gently lubricating his arse. The thoughts of this morning flooded back and he moved his fingers down between his legs, coaxing his sperm to an eagerly awaiting rear.

It took all his willpower to not unzip his pants, grab his cock and masturbate right there on the back door step. If a letter could do this to Charles, then he was sure as hell that he wanted to follow the rabbit hole, his wife's hole and his nine-inch cock fucking that tight arse hole of hers. Reluctantly he stopped fingering himself and moved the plant pot to take the second letter. Before opening it he looked around for the house key, but couldn't find it. Charles didn't know why, because he had already decided to 'take the red pill', but still tried the door handle, He heard a faint noise, but it was firmly locked. "She knew I would take the letter," he thought to himself. Eleanor had already taken control of him from the moment she had stuck it to the door.

The second letter was not addressed to 'Charles', but instead 'MY SEX TOY!'

Excited, nervous and with the release of another wave of pre-cum he unfolded the second note and started reading...

Dear Sex Toy,

By opening this letter you have agreed to <u>MY</u> rules and are now committed to pleasuring ME. You are now mine, you are my fuck toy and you will fulfil your role to open our relationship.

To ensure you understand your purpose, you are now commanded to remove all of your clothes, except for the latex undies that you are wearing. You will leave them where you are now standing.

Charles did as the letter instructed and undressed, removing his jacket and shirt and feeling the slight autumn breeze on his skin. Next came the shoes and socks and then he unbuckled his belt, savouring the eroticism as he slowly unzipped his pants, letting them drop to the floor. He couldn't resist another quick rub over his bulge as he continued to flow the instructions from his wife.

You will now walk to the bottom of the garden and stand in front of the garden shed. Once there you will touch that swelling you will certainly have. You will *rub your arse cheeks, your cock and your arse hole. I want that cum of yours worked into your skin. But, you will <u>NOT</u> put your hands inside your latex panties!*

Only moments ago he was performing the same act, but this time he was almost naked, and the touch of soft damp grass under his bare feet and the autumn breeze gently excited his nipples. Gently he caressed and rubbed his dick with one hand and fingered his arse with the other. With each stroke, pre-cum oozed from the tip of his cock and he could feel with each push of his finger that he was penetrating further, and further inside. Gradually he squatted down to gain better access, and the tightening of the latex around his balls began to squeeze the fresh cum in the direction of his widening hole. The gentle parting of his arse muscles as lubricated latex finger penetrated was far too much and Charles could not keep the growing deep orgasm under control. His muscles clamped around his index finger and he looked down and watched the explosion beneath the latex, feeling the warmth of his sperm trickled down his cock and under his balls. He withdrew his finger and then pushed a fresh load of warm cum back inside.

Charles shuddered, his calf muscles twitched, and his arse and cock were in spasms; never before had he ejaculated with such intensity. He just stood there, out of breath and shaking as a couple more spasms followed originating from the anal depths. He bent down and picked up the note that he had dropped, enjoying the spread of warm liquid as the latex stretched.

Now that you have finished playing with yourself you will shower with the garden hose. The cold water will calm you down, and I DON'T want you to cum. You will not remove those undies because you are almost ready to begin your purpose in life.

Now, face away from the shed and do not turn around. You will be summoned shortly!

Eleanor xxx

"Fuck! I've already broken the second rule." Charles muttered to himself as he turned on the hose pipe. "Jesus, that's damn fucking cold!" he gasped as the freezing water hit his naked body. Quickly he showered himself down to avoid getting too cold. He stood there for a while, shivering whilst waiting for his summons. It was quite dark by now and the moon was slowly passing the side of the house casting its silvery glow on the back garden. "This is getting past a joke," he mumbled to himself, as he began to stamp his numb feet and blow on his hands to try and get some warmth. '"Fuck!" it was cold and any excitement Charles still clung to was rapidly fading.

"When would she appear?" He questioned, but as if in answer he heard the unmistakeable sound of high heel shoes on the pathway behind him.

As the footsteps drew closer his excitement returned. He wanted to turn and watch his beautiful wife walking towards him, bathed in moonlight and wearing the open crotch latex panties, suspender belt and stockings she had bought from the sex shop. He wanted to lay his eyes on the woman who was now the sexually dominating one in their relationship. "I couldn't break another rule could I?" he asked himself.

Eleanor stood behind him, and Charles could feel her rapid breathing behind him. He wondered if she had been watching. He jumped as two hands moved up the back of his thighs, rubbed his buttocks, gently pushing them apart as they moved around his waist and grabbed his excited cock. She began kissing the back of his neck, massaging his cock with one hand and balls with the other. Charles moved backwards, pressing her closer to his rear. She began to run his hands down her arms and found she was wearing long latex gloves which were smooth and delicately oiled. Charles let out a groan in excitement and pleasure as his hands met her latex fingers on his dick.

She responded by pulling him closer. 'Thanks Charles for agreeing', she whispered in his ear.

Just as he was about to respond, "Shhh..." she continued, "There's no need for you to speak. I wanted to say how happy I am you chose to accept my offer. I love you and life will now be much more pleasurable with me in charge." And with that she pulled down hard on the latex sheath, her other hand tugging at his balls, forcing his cock to stretch to its maximum size and pushing his balls down and back between his legs.

"But now 'MY SEX TOY' you're ready to be disciplined."

She removed her hands from her husband's body and stepped backwards.

"Turn around and face me 'SEX TOY'!" she commanded, "And keep your eyes closed. For your disobedience for trying the back door to check if it was unlocked, you will not look at me again tonight! Do you understand?"

Charles nodded his head.

"How the hell did she know I'd tried the front door?' He thought, closing his eyes and turning around to face her.

"Good," Eleanor smirked, "now hold still!"

Charles couldn't believe how excited he was to receive his first consequence for disobeying. She began to pull something over the top of his head. The now familiar smell of latex became evident as she slid what he could only presume was a mask over his face. Once on, she zipped up the back and Charles felt the tightening of the latex on his skin and around my neck. The mask felt slightly thicker than the undies and appeared to be fusing as it warmed to his skin. There were holes for his nose, and the mouth left completely open. His hearing was slightly muffled and his eyes covered.

She then kissed him, thrusting her tongue deep into his mouth. As soon as Charles tried to return her kiss she withdrew.

"You also broke another rule tonight, didn't you? - and this one is much more serious."

"Rule number 2." He confessed.

"Yes, you are to pleasure me TOY," she reprimanded.

Eleanor began to put pressure on his head and pushed him down. "Pleasure me SEX TOY!" she commanded.

His masked face moved down her body, brushing past the suspender belt. He stuck out his tongue, licking her as he continued to move down. As he got to the top of her panties the scent of her pussy juices filled his nostrils and then the taste of her flooded into his mouth as her latex lips opened and filled me with warm wet flesh.

As she pushed his face into her cunt, so that his tongue could penetrate further and savour her sweet juices, he could just about hear what she was saying.

"You'll soon be my perfect little fuck toy." She laughed.

CHARLES MEETS HIS HOT WIFE'S 'NEW FRIENDS'

Charles lay there watching his wife on her hands and knees getting fucked by Pamela with a huge strap-on whilst her husband, Edward continued to massage Charles back. Eleanor groaned in pleasure with each penetration of the dildo into her wet cunt and in return Edward slowly massaged further down Charles's well-oiled body with a vibrating dildo, stopping at the base of his spine with its head pressing down to gently part his buttocks.

It had been about just over an hour since Charles had met Barbra in the back garden, and had taken the couple's relationship entirely into her own hands. As soon as they had entered the house she removed the latex mask her husband was wearing and introduced him to Pamela and Edward. Charles had indeed been fantasising about many things today, but he hadn't even thought about bringing another couple into their sex life. But that was earlier today and the last eleven hours had already proved to be full of beautiful surprises.

"Darling, this is my friend Pamela, and her gorgeous husband, Edward."

Charles just nodded looking at both of them in shock, surprise and genuine sexual curiosity.

"I think we have awakened a curious side of him he didn't know he had," Eleanor laughed as she noticed his cock.

"Or has denied he had," Pamela remarked.

"Charles, just a little reminder… the same rules apply," Eleanor continued, "especially the second one. Anyhow, go with Pamela to the shower so she can get you prepared, but no touching until you're invited to do so!"

With that, Pamela took Charles by the hand and led him upstairs to the shower, leaving Eleanor alone with Edward.

Once in the shower, Pamela proceeded to help Charles remove the latex pants that he had been wearing for most of the day. The sudden nakedness, combined with having a total another woman undressing was exhilarating.

"Oh, you're quite a mess down there, aren't you?" She commented, tugging the pants down his hips and revealing his raging hard cock.

She turned on the shower and pushed him under the warming water, and started to wash his naked body. It was incredible, the feeling of warm soapy water on his skin, and the gentle touch of Pamela's hands as she washed the inside of his thighs and up to his ball and eagerly awaiting cock. Raising his arms above his head, she gently washed the rest of his body.

"Now it's my turn," she smiled as she handed him the bottle of shower gel and the flannel, "Start at the top and slowly make your way down."

Charles started with her neck and shoulders and moved down her back following the stream of lather flowing down over her curved arse and disappearing between her legs. She shifted her stance a little to allow him access to her inner thighs, so he continued down her beautiful long legs and when he reached her feet Charles retraced his steps back up to her shoulders. Pamela turned back round to face him, and her erect nipples immediately caught his attention. He applied more soap and lathered her big tits, taking good care to wash and excite her nipples with the texture of the flannel. Working the cloth down her body, he stopped while he wondered if he should or should not attempt to remove her white panties, which had become transparent, revealing her smooth pussy underneath.

"Hold on," Pamela said, turning around, and pushing her arse onto his erection. She took hold of his hands and held one on her tit and placed the other one down the front of her panties

"Slide your hand under Charles, and give me a good fucking wash."

She then began to move my hands and gently moved her hips, pushing his cock in between her arse cheeks. He played with her tits, washed her pussy and gyrated until she let out a small moan as she climaxed.

"Mmm…that's much better," She panted, "And now it's time to get you ready." With that Pamela turned back to face Charles and planted a short passionate kiss on his lips.

"Thanks, Sweetheart… It was really nice to meet you. I'll look forward to having your big cock deep inside me the next time." She winked.

"What? There's going to be a next time?" Charles thought to himself, while she washed the remaining soap of their bodies and then dried them both dry with a bath towel. She placed her arm around his waist, snuggled up and led Charles out of the bathroom.

They made their way back downstairs to the living room and as they entered Charles stopped in surprise. Whilst Charles and Pamela were getting to know each other in the shower, his wife and Edward were doing the same. Somewhere deep down Charles had expected to see Edward fucking his wife with his huge cock or at least see her taking as much of his dick as she could in her filthy mouth, but he had not expected to see Edward on all fours, with his underpants pulled down to his ankles and Eleanor kneeling behind him pounding his arse with a strap-on.

Pamela let go of Charles's hand and kissed Eleanor passionately on the lips. She moved in front of her husband, slid her wet panties off her hips, spread her pussy lips wide open and pushed her pussy into his face. Each push of the dildo in his arse pushed him deeper into his wife's cunt. Pamela pulled his head into her while Eleanor fucked him harder and harder. Her breathing became more rapid and Charles could see she was so close to climaxing, and he too was close as he watched the erotic scene in front of him. He didn't quite know which was more exciting; his wife with the strap-on fucking the arse of a total stranger, the smooth pussy of another woman thrust into the face of her husband or the extremely large, cum soaked cock of Edward beckoning to be sucked and emptied. Charles cock was now painfully hard, dribbling pre-cum off his own in sync with Edward's.

He wanted to be in his position, he wanted his arse fucked and invaded by his wife's strap-on whilst tasting the sweet juices of Pamela's cunt ...... or sucking on that monster cock!

Eleanor let out a final groan signalling the arrival of a well-needed orgasm. This in return pushed her dildo deeper into Edward with a sharp jolt. Pamela arched her back as she exploded in Edward's mouth and Edward shot his load up towards his navel and across the massage table.

"Fuck!" Charles murmured out loud feeling the explosive release in the air of three colliding orgasms. "Fuck!" he repeated as he watched the long length of the dildo slowly withdraw out of Edward's bum. The contracting sphincter muscles were forced to expand once more as the bulbous head of the strap-on finally forced its way out of his hole, teasing a final spurt of cum out of his cock. His arse muscle's twitched a couple of times trying to close the gap, but the constant pounding had opened him wide and it would take a while for his beautiful ring to return to its normal size.

*****

Charles lay there watching his wife on her hands and knees getting fucked by Pamela with a huge strap-on whilst her husband, Edward continued to massage Charles back. Eleanor groaned in pleasure with each penetration of the dildo into her wet cunt and in return

Edward slowly massaged further down Charles's well-oiled body with a vibrating dildo, stopping at the base of his spine with its head pressing down to gently part his buttocks.

He changed his position and moved around in front of Charles. His big cock, now fully erect, but still kept under wraps in the tight underpants, was just inches away from Charles's face.

"Have you ever sucked cock before?" He asked while Charles admired how huge and wet he was.

"No, never," Charles replied shaking his head.

"Mmm…" was all Edward replied, brushing the head of his dick past Charles' lips and pushing the vibrating dildo further down his crack.

Charles let out an unexpected groan as he felt a slight stickiness on his lips.

Edward then brushed his cock past Charles's lips again and pulled the dildo back up his crack. This time Charles licked his lips to taste Edward's juice, but he only had the slightest taste, and he wanted more.

Edward pulled away. "Remove your underwear, Charles, if you want more."

Charles didn't hesitate, he brought both his arms around, slid his hands up his muscled thighs and up to his hips. He tucked his fingers into his waistband and slid his briefs down. Edward's cock stood there to attention then twitched as he clenched his muscles as a signal to continue.

Charles caressed the underneath of Edward's sack then grabbed his cock. He couldn't believe that he was actually holding another man's cock in his hand; in fact, he couldn't believe how much of a turn on it was holding another man's cock.

Edward slowly began to move forwards and backwards, jerking his cock in Charles's hand. He matched his movements with the dildo, moving it closer and closer to Charles's arse hole.

In response, Charles moved his other hand behind him and slowly pulled him closer. He moved his hand further up his cock to feel his damp head, his pre-cum adding natural lubricant as he continued to masturbate. More cum came as he pushed the dildo into the entrance of Charles's hole who moved his hips up to greet the long-awaited fucking.

Charles was wanking off another man, pulling his incredibly sized cock closer and closer to his mouth whilst he was pushing a vibrating dildo into his eagerly awaiting arse, no wonder he was almost ready to shoot his load there and then.

"Take his cock CUCKBOY!" Charles heard his wife command, "Take it now!"

Charles opened his mouth wide and swallowed the sperm covered head of his shaft. In return, someone applied a generous amount of lube and Edward slid the dildo inside him. His tight asshole still fought to keep the dildo out, but the lube forced it past his sphincter. Edward thrust his cock further into Charles' mouth and the dildo further inside him, back and forth slid his cock and the dildo as Charles's muscles relaxed and accepted the penetration easier. He moved his hips in rhythm to his movements and to ride the dildo in ecstasy as it pounded his prostate. His mouth was full of cock dribbling cum and he wanted more, even though he could not take all of him, still, Charles reached around behind him and pulled him closer to him. The sensations in his tight butt were getting more and more intense and he could feel Edward's cock beginning to expand as he got closer to orgasm. The thought of having Edward explode in Charles's mouth was cut short when he suddenly removed the dildo.

"Now it's my turn." Eleanor interrupted. He then felt the head of her huge strap on rest at his entrance.

Edward put his hand on the back of Charles's head and pushed him closer to take more of his dick.

"Now you will become my perfect bisexual-fuck toy." She continued while plunging deep inside her husband.

Edward let out an almighty groan and instantly exploded in Charles's mouth, his hot sticky cum forcing itself down his throat.

SOME OLD FRIENDS
DOWN AT THE OFFICE.

A good few weeks had passed since Eleanor had taken the reins of the couple's sex life. They still hooked up with Pamela and Edward a couple of times a week, and both ladies had taking turns stretching Charles's arse to a reasonable size, comfortably accommodating the variety of rubber cocks and strap-on dildo's they used to screw him, while Edward thrust his big cock down his throat, which Charles craved more and more.

During this time, Charles had never had Edward's impressive cock fucking his arse - Eleanor had not allowed it. Charles constantly imagined him rubbing the tip of his cock against his hole, tantalising him as he gently lubricated the entrance with his pre-cum. He was desperate, and couldn't wait any longer so he pushed backwards onto his dick, flexing his rear muscles so they opened to engulf him and then sheer ecstasy as it slid inside, forcing the whole length of his fuck inside with one push until Charles could feel his balls banging against his arse.

Charles and Eleanor's wedding anniversary was only weeks away, and he knew that she had something special planned, but the rules didn't permit Charles to ask or even mention it.

But tonight, Eleanor had permitted Charles and Edward to play alone, with her there, fully in charge pleasure, of course.

Charles prayed that he would be getting fucked by Edward's big dick, the mere thought of it had already given him a raging hard-on, and his arse on fire as it continuously contracted around the snap butt plug, held tightly with latex panties which Eleanor inserted there that morning.

"Thank God the latex sheath is housing all the spunk I have already released this morning and doesn't show through my trousers. Another big thank you to the desk I'm sitting behind to cover up my evident bulge as there are clients in the office!" Charles smiled to himself.

"And that - I think concludes our business, Charles." Said the auburn haired lady, "That just leave the formalities of you checking over the paperwork and sending them to our solicitor by the end of the week."

Shit! Meeting over and his cock was still erect.

"Just one question," Charles replied in order to gain some extra ease down time, "Could you confirm the payment and payee details on the final page as a matter of course?"

The clients turned to the final page and read the details. "Everything seems correct," they confirmed a little too quickly.

He gathered the papers together, his erection slowly subsiding, and placed them in a document folder.

"They should be with your solicitor, first thing Friday morning," Charles confirmed, putting the folder to one side, before standing up and reaching out to shake their hands, but not before he noticed that they both had taken a quick glance at the bulge in his grey trousers as he stood.

"Nice doing business with you Charles, and give our love to your wife. You both must call round one evening for dinner and a few drinks,"

"Yes, that'd be nice - look forward to it," Charles answered.

"Great, I'll give her a call to arrange a date."

Charles walked around his desk and opened the door for his two female clients, Mary and Anne.

"Really good to see you both again," he said kissing them both on the cheek while picturing these two old friends and his wife with strap-on in hand as they take it in turns to ruthlessly fuck him over the dinner table. "I'm sure Eleanor would be very excited to meet up again for dinner."

"Probably not as excited as you are."

With that they left arm in arm, leaving Charles blushing at the office door, **"Shit! Shit! Shit!"** He thought.

DARLING, WHY WAS YOUR COCK SO HARD TODAY?

Charles arrived home later that day and was greeted by his sexy wife in the kitchen.

"Hi darling, you had a good day at work?" she asked closing the door behind him.

"Hmm... it's been interesting," he replied kissing her.

Eleanor wrapped her arms around his waist. "Yes, so I've heard," she smiled, "We've received a dinner invitation from Mary and Anne,"

"Wow, that was quick," he said, "I didn't expect them to call so soon."

Moving one of her hands down the front of Charles's trousers she began to lightly rub. "They also told me that you appeared to be somewhat distracted during the meeting." His cock immediately responded to her touch. "Do you want to tell me what you were thinking about?" She teased.

"Well..." he began, "I just couldn't stop thinking about being alone with Edward tonight with you in charge, telling us what to do," He lifted her short skirt above her hips, and began rubbing his bulge against her white panties.

"Continue what you're telling me," she ordered.

"I'm looking forward to being his submissive slut this evening," Charles continued.

Eleanor pushed him back a little and unzipped his trousers, releasing his sheathed erection.

"This feels extremely wet and full of sperm," she teased, stretching the latex sheath up and down his cum covered dick, "anyhow, please continue."

"I just kept imagining kneeling down in front of Edward with that big cock hanging between his legs only a few inches from my face. His hand slowly pulling back the foreskin of his dick, and revealing his swollen head leaking pre-cum."

Eleanor let her skirt fall to the floor, and thrust her pussy against her husband's dick. "Continue," she ordered again.

"I can feel his heat as he brushes his cock against my eagerly awaiting lips so I can taste his fresh spunk. Edward then puts his hand on my head and I open my dirty mouth to let him push his big cock between my lips and down my throat."

Eleanor began to breathe harder, rubbing herself against her husband, faster and rougher. He could feel the lace of her panties against the sheath, adding further stimulation to his already overexcited dick.

"He places his other hand on the back of my head, forcing me deeper onto his cock, he rocks my head back and forth along his veins shaft, his tip banging against the back of my throat making me gag. There is no way I can stop him, my mouth is his fuck toy and I'm his dirty little cock whore."

Eleanor backed herself against the kitchen wall and jumped in his arms. "Charles, put your cock in me and fuck me now!" she demanded.

Tightly he held her against him, pulling her knickers to the side, feeling how wet she was and placing his latex cock against her soaking wet hole.

"Edward pushes me further onto his big cock," Charles moaned as he slid his rubber cock into her. "Further and further until I can't take anymore,"

"Fuck me you dirty bastard," Eleanor gasped as he plunged the rest of his cock deep into her, "Suck Edward's cock until he explodes."

"I feel Edward's breathing getting harder," Eleanor picked up the pace and started groaning loudly.

"His thrusting becomes more forceful, trying to squeeze every inch of his cock in my mouth," Eleanor rocked her hips, pushing Charles as deep inside her as she could.

"I can sense he is close, building up to an explosive climax, his balls clench, his shaft twitches and stiffens to the max," S arched her back, wrapping her legs around me and forcing me closer.

His cock followed suit, balls clenched, shaft stiffened. "Edward explodes, I can feel the warmth of his seed flooding my mouth and running down the back of my throat."

Eleanor clamped her pussy around his cock as she flooded her cunt with her own climax. Reaching behind Charles, she slid her fingers over his grey trousers and forcefully pushed the butt plug hard against his prostate. Instantly he ejaculated in the sheath; the flood of his own warm cum coated his cock and balls. His arse muscles contracted around the plug simultaneously trying to expel it and pull it deeper inside.

Eleanor snuggled into his neck, trying to catch her breath. "That was fucking hot..." she gasped between breaths, "Now I understand why Mary and Anne knew you were distracted today."

There was silence for a moment while Eleanor thought. "It looks like I really need to find a new direction for you both tonight to beat this orgasm."

"Just let me have his cock inside my arse, PLEASE!" Charles thought to himself as he caught his breath.

"Come with me," Eleanor said, taking Charles by the hand and leading him upstairs to the bedroom.

He pulled down her soaking panties, amazed at how wet they were considering that it was just her juice. She removed his cock out of the sheath, glistening and sticky with all the cum released over the day and the recent climax. The cool air seducing it back to a semi hard state. This time she bent down and began to suck just as Charles had imagined doing to Edward. As she sucked, slowly she peeled down his latex briefs and gently tugged on the butt plug. His arse was still on fire and would not relinquish the plug without some effort. Eleanor continued sucking his cum covered cock and tugging, teasing both my cock and ass with her actions. Then with a sudden jerk, she yanked out the plug. There was an immediate sensual pain as the plug forced itself past my contracted sphincter driving the reminder of cum out of my cock.

"Mmm, that tastes so fucking good," Eleanor replied as she sucked the last few drops of spunk from her husband's dick.

She placed the plug into the sheath and began to rub the plug up and down, lubricating it with his spent seed as she had wanked his cock earlier.

"I want you to cover your fingers with the remainder of your cum from the sheath and lube up my ass with it," Eleanor ordered as she turned around, bent over and exposed her smooth arsehole to him.

He lubricated his fingers and gently began to massage her right hole in gentle circular motions. She soon started to move her hips in rhythm to his caresses, encouraging him to move closer to her centre. As he moved towards her beautiful butt hole he felt her relax, her arse opening as she gently pushed against his fingers, allowing him to lube her inner rim.

"Now insert the plug," she demanded.

Charles placed the plug against her glistening hole and, without waiting for him to push it further; suddenly she pushed back, the bulbous shaft instantly disappearing and held in place by its base.

"Mmm... that feels better filled with your Edward fantasy spunk soaked butt plug," she said clenching her muscles around it, "Now time for a shower, then dinner and preparations for this evening, cock-boy."

Then they showered, enjoying the tenderness of washing each other after the erotic foreplay earlier. Once dressed in casual clothes they prepared dinner and sat down to eat. Chatting about their day, but all talk of tonight was strictly out of bounds.

Charles admired his beautiful new wife; the past few weeks had certainly been a total turnaround of not only true sex life but also their faltering couple. By taking control and making sure that her directing persona with Edward and Pamela was also harmonised by her gentleness when they were alone, Eleanor had ensured that both of them discovered and enjoyed her non-selfish sexual liberation. In a sense, her control had also liberated him from the dominating husband that he had become instead of being the man she married. He admired the way she had never given up on their relationship; respecting that Charles should be thinking about her pleasure, how she felt and how he could please her.

"Edward will be here around 10 o'clock tonight after he's taken Pamela to some young guy's apartment that she's fucking," Eleanor said getting up from her a chair to clear the plates and cutlery from the dining table. "So, that should give us a few hours to enjoy ourselves before the fun really starts," she continued with a sly smirk on her face, "come on darling, grab your coat we're going out."

"Where are we going?" Charles asked.

"Just somewhere that'll put us in the mood for tonight."

"But, I'm already in the mood," he grinned.

"I know, but I was thinking of getting myself more in the mood, an idea I had today which I would like to see if it could happen."

"Hmmm… that sounds intriguing! If it's anything like your other ideas recently, I'm sure you will manage to make it happen."

"What you waiting for? Grab your coat," she said tossing him the car keys, "and you're driving. I could do with a few drinks to pluck up some courage."

Charles was intrigued, "Courage?" He repeated, "but -" He stopped, looked into her emerald green eyes and saw she had no doubt that she would put her plan into action. The drinks were still part of the reserved Eleanor that Charles had married, a sincere part of her, which he hoped she would never lose. He grabbed his coat, closed the locked the back door, and walked arm in arm to the car, enjoying the closeness they shared, but in the back of his mind he was thinking, "What the fuck did she now have in mind?"

They drove the few miles into town, his mind only partly on the road. "So where are we going?" He asked, glancing at Eleanor. She looked radiant, he thought. Whether it was the thought of embarking on her new idea, the fantastic sex they had just had, or simply the butt plug inserted in her arse, Charles had no idea, but she really did look so full of happiness.

"Head for the main street and pull in as soon as you see a somewhere to park."

Eleanor was playing this one very close to her chest, not giving any clues away. Charles pulled in as soon as he saw a place to park. They got out the car and Eleanor walked around to Charles and linked her arm in his.

"Thanks darling for doing this," she beamed.

"I haven't a clue what's going on," he smiled back at her, "but if it is anything like your other ideas I'm sure we'll both love it."

They kissed and Eleanor led the way.

The evening with Edward was still playing over and over in the back of Charles's dirty mind, but here he was enjoying a stroll down the street with Eleanor, with the final warmth of a beautiful autumn evening setting behind them and heading for - well, he had no fucking idea whatsoever!

Gently he was pulled away from his romantic dream as Eleanor tugged him to the right and into the *Royal Oak*. They hadn't been there for a long while, a regular haunt a few years back and it was also the place where they had enjoyed first ever romantic meal.

"Grab us a couple of drinks and I'll try and find a table in the garden."

"Sure, any particular drink?" He asked.

"Have a look at the cocktails, and surprise me with the one with the name which grabs your attention."

Charles made his way to the bar while Eleanor headed toward the beer garden. He watched her navigate her way through the people, gently touching the shoulders of both males and females, smiling at them as she squeezed past. This, Charles was certain, was part of her plan, knowing that she would be receiving some subtle attention, as she made her way through. He was quite aroused to see she was turning heads as she moved among the people. Especially from a few men who, like me, were drawn to the way her butt swayed seductively under the short blue dress that she was wearing, the silk accentuating her beautiful curves. Even more aroused by the knowledge that out of view to all, with each rhythmic sway of her hips the butt plug would be gently massaging her hole.

Once she disappeared amongst the crowd Charles looked at the cocktail list behind the bar and instantly saw the cocktail that he would get her.

He made his way outside and found Eleanor sitting at the table with Mary and Anne!

"Hi Charles, good to see that you've calmed down since this morning," Mary said flashing a wicked smile.

He put the drinks down and kissed each of the ladies on their cheek. "Good evening ladies... Erm… I must admit that I'm rather embarrassed about that," he blushed.

"Oh, don't be," Mary laughed, "Just look at you two... you both look like newlyweds. Whatever you're doing together, it must be working."

"And Eleanor, you're looking as beautiful as ever," Anne said raising her glass towards Eleanor.

Eleanor beamed and took a sip of the cocktail. "Mmm, that's good darling..."

"Can I get you two ladies, a drink?" Charles asked.

"I'll have what Eleanor is drinking," said Mary.

"Me too, whatever it is," added Anne.

"*Dark Desires'*," Charles replied starting to laugh and feeling his face flush again.

"Well Charles, quite appropriate don't you think," Mary said looking at him straight in the eye as she reached over to place her hand on top of Eleanor's.

Eleanor looked startled and then started laughing. "*Dark Desires'* all round please Charles," she said with a wink, which he could not help feel was a wink of accomplishment indicating that her plan had been set in motion.

He went inside to order drinks. "What the fuck was Eleanor up to?" he thought, "Surely it couldn't be a coincidence that Mary and Anne had telephoned to arrange a dinner date and then they 'accidentally' meet up here as it was too shorter notice for dinner tonight?" Obviously, Eleanor plan involved them, but in which capacity Charles could only guess, and knowing his wife and her plans this was going to be interesting, painfully frustrating in anticipation, but very interesting.

He returned with the cocktails to a round of applause from the three ladies.

"Thank you, Charles." Anne said, "Eleanor's just been telling us about your little secret,"

"Little secret?" He stammered, feeling slightly uncomfortable with where this could lead.

"Yes, how you two still look so much in love, we can practically feel the chemistry radiating out from you both."

"Don't worry," Mary laughed, "Eleanor hasn't gone into all the horny details,"

"But she has asked us a favour," Anne added.

"Favour?" Now he was totally confused.

"Darling," Eleanor answered, "I've been explaining to Mary and Anne that you've been paying more attention to me lately, making me feel so loved, so special and also so desirable."

Charles was undoubtedly stuck for words wondering where this was now going. "Oh right – yes, that's right." He laughed awkwardly.

"I also told them why you were distracted this morning."

"You did?" He asked, looking down slightly and feeling like a misbehaved school boy that had been caught doing something he shouldn't have.

His teasing wife loved every second of this, watching him wondering what had been said, what was going on and feeling extremely uncomfortable.

"Sorry if I have embarrassed you again, but Mary and Anne have kindly agreed to help."

Charles turned to them, still stuck for words.

"We know It's your wedding anniversary in a couple of weeks and you want to buy something special for Eleanor but don't want her to see it before the big evening," explained Anne.

"They've agreed to go shopping with you and model the lingerie and dress that I'll wear for our anniversary evening," Eleanor explained, "And that way you'll see how it looks and can also imagine how sexy I'll look in it."

Finally, Charles started to understand his wife's plan. Giving Mary and Anne just enough information about their sex life to interest them, show them how happy and open they had become whilst also inadvertently or deliberately tapping into his earlier daydream. Eleanor was not overly flirtatious with Mary, but the way Mary was tenderly caressing Eleanor's petite hand did suggest that she had sensed how attracted Eleanor was to her. He had no way of knowing for sure, and possibly was way off track, but his wife had now manoeuvred the both of them into an extremely arousing situation with the opportunity for the couple to further their relationship.

"Is that okay with you, darling?" Eleanor asked.

"Sure," he said, "it sounds like a once in a lifetime shopping trip I can finally enjoy!" he joked.

"Christ, it's been years since Mary and I have paraded around in underwear for a man," Anne laughed, "It would make our next office meeting quite interesting Charles, don't you think?"

"Bets on to see who makes him blush first," Mary teased.

"Or aroused," Eleanor continued.

"Erm... ladies I'm still here," Charles said light-heartedly.

"Maybe in body, but I'm quite sure we all know where your mind is right now," taunted Mary taunted, making the other two ladies laugh while Charles just sat grinning and blushing.

They looked at him and started laughing again. Eleanor was crying, thoroughly enjoying the moment, the company, and most likely sowing the seeds of her plan.

At the end of the evening, they all walked back towards the car, having said their goodbyes, plus the arranging the shopping adventure for a week on Saturday.

"Well... it looks like the drinks helped with the courage tonight," Charles laughed, hugging his wife as they walked to the car.

"Yes," she replied returning the hug.

"And... did everything go to plan?" He asked

"Plan, darling? I just wanted to show them how happy we are, and maybe a little flirting with them both."

"So tonight's plan was in fact just to flirt with Mary and Anne?"

"Yes... I suppose it was." She smiled.

"But, what about the lingerie shopping?" He added.

"Just a little improvisation. You have to admit you're going to have a great time," she replied, poking him in the ribs.

"Sure am, but why did you want to meet Mary and Anne tonight to get you in the mood?"

She stopped with her hands on her curved hips. "You really have no idea, do you?"

"No," Charles replied slightly confused.

"Charles, I love you, I love fucking you with my strap-on, I love it when you suck

Edward's cock and he gets off in your mouth and I love the taste of his spunk on your lips when you kiss me. I also love having sex with Pamela, sliding her dildo inside my pussy, taking me from behind and having her fucking my arse, but most of all, I adore you watching me being taken by her."

Charles was getting more and more excited with her words and also the fact she was being honest with him.

"It is special when we make love, the intimacy, the erotic and also the risk," she said, sliding one hand down the front of his trousers and with her other hand she moved his hand under her short red dress.

"Can you feel how much I'm excited by the thought of us and our wonderful sex life," she whispered while directing Charles's fingers along her clit and massaging the tip of his index finger against her soaking lace panties and the base of the butt plug. "I really want us to enjoy everything together. I want you to be fucked, and be with me when I'm fucked, by the women and men that I find attractive."

Charles was ready to cum there and then in her hand as she confided in me one of her desires. She grabbed my cock at the base to prevent me from shooting. She removed my hand from under her skirt and lightly brushed my fingers over my lips and down my chin. The intoxicatingly sweet smell of her sex drifted between us.

"You have to admit darling, Mart and Anne are two very sexy women."

"Yes," Charles nodded.

"Don't tell me you haven't fantasised about them?"

"Yes," he admitted as there was no point hiding it from her.

"Fantasised about them fucking you from both ends with dildos?"

"Yes," he confirmed, "Eleanor, you know me so well."

There was a short pause in the couple's conversation as Charles thought about tonight. He had no idea what his wife was thinking about but was curious to find out and see if he could push her even further and expand on her revelation.

"Apart from the fact they are so fucking sexy," Charles said, breaking the silence, "but, why Mary and Anne? They've been our friends for a good few years now and there's been no flirting before tonight... not that I'm aware of..."

"Well... we haven't really seen them since our new lifestyle, have we?"

"Yes, that's true,"

"I'd just taken a shower when they telephoned, and... to be honest, I was trying on some new clothes for this evening, which had arrived earlier, and I was quite turned on."

"And?"

"Well, we got chatting, and I was kinda enjoying the way the tight suppleness of the latex felt against my skin... Every movement I made was accentuated. I was kind of paying attention to Anne, but I was so horny that I could feel the warmth of my pussy seeping through the latex as I ran my fingers over it. I closed my eyes and listened to the sexiness of Anne's voice on the phone, imagining she was next to me and that ignited an old feeling that I had..."

"So, I take it that you've been attracted to them for a while?" Charles questioned.

"Yes darling, but the old me denied those feelings."

Charles smiled and looked into his wife's beautiful emerald green eyes. "I love the new you," he said kissing her, caressing her curved arse and pulling her against his hard cock.

She put her head back so Charles could kiss her neck, one of the most sensitive parts of her body. She murmured a little as he delicately brushed his warm lips against her flesh.

"Charles, there's more," she whispered

"More?"

"There was an unexpected outcome tonight, and it was something that I hadn't quite expected."

Charles continued his kisses, but she broke away and looked directly at him. "They agreed to the favour only on one condition."

"Which is?" He asked.

"Charles, I have no fucking idea," she laughed, "and to think I thought I was in control of the evening!"

"Now get your sexy butt in the car!" she ordered, "you have a fuck date with Edward, and I intend that you keep it."

They drove back home in total silence, he knew well enough when Eleanor was in this mindset, his role was to submit to her, rules had been established and he was to obey. He reversed the car into the garage, pulled on the handbrake and turned the ignition off. Eleanor grabbed his arm as he was about to get out of the car.

"Thanks again for tonight," she smiled.

He smiled and nodded, "Well you certainly know how to keep our marriage alive and kicking." He went to kiss her, but Eleanor lightly slapped him away and got out of the car.

ELEANOR & CHARLES BOTH FINALLY ENJOY EDWARD'S COCK.

"Charles, take your clothes off," Eleanor ordered with a look that said she wouldn't ask twice.

Quickly he stripped and stood naked in front of her, slightly cold, but with a full erection. Sexily she walked up to him, grabbed his balls and began to squeeze.

"So tell me - how much of Edward do you want this evening?" she whispered whilst nibbling his earlobe.

His dick twitched, straining the foreskin as much as it could. "I want all of him," he admitted, letting out a short gasp as she began to squeeze a little harder.

"All of him?" She repeated, pushing his cock down and back between his legs.

"Yes," he gasped, as she scrapped the sensitive head of his cock with her red painted fingernails.

"You're going have to work hard for it tonight," she said resting the tip of her finger on his lips. He could smell the heat of his juice on her finger and began to suck, pushing it inside his mouth and relishing the taste of his own sperm.

"Good little *Cock boy*." She said, "Now get yourself upstairs and shower and I'll be there shortly to inspect you. Make sure you pay particular attention to your arse - because it is going to be well abused this evening."

A naked Charles hurried upstairs with the taste of his salty sperm on his lips, a set of painful balls and an erection leading the way. Secretly hoping that tonight would be the night when his arse would be seriously abused by his lover's cock.

As instructed, he showered, paying particular attention to his behind. He made sure he was groomed, his balls and arse crack shaved smooth and ready for a good fucking. Minutes later Eleanor appeared and inspected while he towelled himself dry.

"Mmm... you're looking rather sexy, and I'm looking forward to seeing that body of yours being used and abused by 'our' friend this evening. Come here, I have a little something for you." She said, holding a small box in one of her hands.

He stepped out of the shower and walked up to her still drying his hair, but as he got closer she put a hand on his chest to stop. She opened the small box so that Charles could see his gift.

"This will help to prolong the evening," she smiled, fastening the leather strap around his waist. The front strap, containing three steel rings welded together in a 'U' shape and a larger unconnected ring banged gently against his cock as she tightened the leather waist strap.

"Don't get too excited," she laughed, applying some lubricating jelly onto his cock and balls.

She took the larger ring and began to slide one of his balls through the ring.

He flinched a bit as the first testicle squeezed through the ring, then she started to push his other through, but this time the aching pain was a little more excruciating as his ball was pushed through the narrowed space of the ring.

"Now to get that cock of yours through before it gets too excited," she chuckled pushing the head of his dick down inside his foreskin. His shaft began to bend as she forced the tip of my foreskin through the remaining space in the ring. Charles was nowhere near fully excited, but hard enough to feel the discomfort as it forced its way under the ring and back up his foreskin. Eleanor simultaneously pushed down on the arc of his shaft and pulled his foreskin. The swollen head forced under the ring then painfully through as she placed the middle of the 'U' shaped rings over the crown and forcefully pushed both of the cock rings down my lubricated shaft.

"Jesus *Fucking* Christ!" He gasped at the pain and the relief as everything finally slipped through the rings.

"Is it uncomfortable?" She asked, feigning concern, and without waiting for any reply she pushed each of his testicles through the outer rings, threaded a strap through the base of the central ring, before pulling it tightly through his legs and between his buttocks where she attached it to the back of the belt.

There was a knock on the door. Edward Charles beamed, causing a further tightness around his cock and balls.

Eleanor went to the door and opened it. "Good evening, Edward," she smiled, greeting him with a sweet kiss on the cheek.

"Good evening, Eleanor," replied Edward returning her kiss, "Howdy, Charles," he nodded, knowing no contact could me made unless Eleanor had given permission to do so, but at least Charles had the benefit of Edward looking him up and down, pausing as he looked at his protruding cock with the additional caging.

Eleanor closed the door, there was a faint click as she locked it - signalling that the evening had begun and the two men were now under her control.

"Boys - Tonight the rules are quite simple - you already know what you can and can't do."

Both men nodded.

"I will direct you as and when I feel fit to do so, but the rest is your evening to freely explore, excite and abuse each other. Do you understand me?"

They both nodded again in confirmation.

"Okay, to get things started, Edward, get undressed and then take Charles into the bathroom and secure his arms above him."

Charles watched as Edward undressed, yet again admiring his toned torso as he removed his white t-shirt. He unbuckled his belt and unzipped his trousers letting them fall to the floor so he could step out of them. He stood in front of Charles, almost naked apart from the white underpants that he was wearing, his erection clearly evident along with the signs of pre-cum soaking through the front of his pants. He slipped them off, releasing his veiny cock which twitched and squeezed more juice from its tip.

Charles turned around and moved towards the shower. He could feel his arse puckering, knowing that Edward was behind him, secretly hoping he would break the rules and force his big cock right up his yearning arse.

Edward took hold of another leather strap, which was hanging on the shower tap, and secured Charles hands together, and lifting his arms above his head to secure them to the hook from the bathroom ceiling. Edward ran his hands down Charles's muscular arms, one hand stopping on the back of his head which he pulled towards him so he could begin kissing him, whilst the other hand continued to brush down the side of

Charles's body, over his hip, and over to the middle of his buttocks. He pushed, bringing their erect cocks together. Charles let out a gasp as Edward's cock twitched against his; the feeling of being bound and secured was such a new direction for him, being unable to touch him, being totally under his control was so fucking exciting.

"Edward!" Eleanor interrupted.

Both men froze, fearing they had done something that they would be disciplined for.

"Take the tube of cream from the shelf and spread it all over Charles's body before you continue."

Edward did as he was told, and smiled when he realised what it was and popped the lid open and squeezed it into his hands. The sudden unmistakable smell of ammonia filled the shower room and Charles immediately realised it was hair removal!

Charles was far from a bear and knowing how he felt having a smooth arse crack and sack, he was really sure he would love having all his body hair removed, especially since it would be Edward who would be applying the cream and washing his body off to reveal my new smooth hairless body.

"Edward, spread the cream all over from the neck down only," grinned Eleanor, "you can untie his arms - I wouldn't want to get some of that stuff on his hair, well, not this evening anyway."

Edward untied Charles's arms and began to rub the hair removal cream on them. He then did under his arms, working down his chest, back and all over his buttocks. He then bent down in front of Charles and applied the cream from his ankles to his dick. Edward stood up, smiled and stepped back towards Eleanor. Charles could feel the cream warming and tighten on his skin, his erection continued to strain against its restraints as he imagined what was to come next.

"My arms are starting to burn slightly."

Edward turned to Eleanor who nodded her head in approval. He started to delicately scrape off the cream and hair from Charles's arms then continued to the rest of his body. Once done, Charles turned on the shower and warm water began to wash over his body. Edward picked up the sponge, soaped it up and rubbed Charles body free from any remaining cream. Slowly but surely his glistening smooth naked body began to emerge as the warm water washed away all his bodily hair.

"Do you like your fuck buddy all smooth, Edward?" Eleanor asked.

"Yes," he replied.

"Would you like to restrain him again and make him your fuck toy?"

"Yes," replied Edward, his veiny cock grew rock hard.

She was sitting on a chair in the corner of the room, nestling on her butt plug and slowly rubbing her soaked panties into her cunt.

"I want you two to make me so fucking horny that I'll want more than my fucking fingers up my cunt to satisfy me tonight," she ordered as she continued to pleasure herself.

Edward immediately turned Charles sideways, got in the shower and began fingering and rimming his arse. Charles could see how excited his wife was watching Edward licking his arse while reaching in front of him and stroking his hand up and down his erect dick, just by the way her pussy lips were opening in response to her touch.

"Well done boys, you're just making me so fucking hot watching you two dirty little cocksuckers," Eleanor said, opening her legs wider and resting them on the arms of the chair before inserting two of her fingers inside her gaping hole and slowly fucking herself. "Edward, suck his cock and jerk him as roughly as you can until he spunks in your mouth," Eleanor ordered, her breathing becoming heavier as she wiggled herself against the butt plug and slipped another finger into her pussy.

Edward didn't hesitate and turned Charles around, grabbed his shaft and pulled whatever skin he could back against the cock ring then plunged the dick deep into his mouth. Charles gasped, both in pain and in ecstasy as he bit down on him and flicked his tongue over his swollen head.

Eleanor continued to rock back and forth on the butt plug, her fingers, wet with her own juices, continued to rapidly slide in and out of her. She raised her hips arched her back; Charles knew she was close. She forced her fingers up her cunt as far as they could go and then sank deeply onto the butt plug, triggering her climax which in return forced my cock as far down Edward's throat as possible. Charles's balls stiffened, painfully expanding against the two steel rings and he exploded in harmony with my wife.

"Edward, come over here and cover my body from the neck down in lubrication," Eleanor ordered as the final tremors of Charles's orgasm ran through him.

Edward moved over to Eleanor, and took the huge tub of lube from the bed and dipped his hand in. Eleanor stood facing her husband, compelling him to watch as Edward moved behind her and began to rub lube over her shoulders and around her neck. Charles was still recovering from Edward's amazing blowjob, his arms were aching slightly from being fastened above his head and his legs still felt a little wobbly, but his cock was springing back into action as Edward laid his hands on his slutwife for the first time.

"Mmm… That's so fucking good - you have one hell of a touch," Eleanor smiled, looking her husband straight in the eyes.

Edward continued to lube down her back, bringing his hands up the side of her body and delicately touching the side of her firm tits. Charles's cock continued to grow to the soft squelching sound of the lube as his hands glided over his wife's body. She raised her arms in the air and Edward's hands continued their journey, lubing up and over the top of her arms, her fingers, which appeared to briefly hold Edward's, then back down the underside of her arms to her armpits.

"Edward, Reach around and lube my tits,"

He grabbed more lube from the tub, and moved closer to her, reaching around her to cover her tits with lube. Charles hung there helpless, unable to join, watching Edward gently massage his wife's tits, pushing them together, reaching under them and teasing her erect glistening nipples.

"So fucking good…" gasped Eleanor as she began to push her body against Edward's and slowly move her hips. He continued down her chest, her stomach and stopped at the top of her shaved pussy. Eleanor groaned and pushed against him further then looked at Charles. "Continue Edward, work your way up my legs then lube my pussy and arse slowly while my husband watches."

Edward bent down and began to work his way up her legs. Charles could do nothing but watch, he noticed the obvious chemistry between them and wondered if she was going to fuck him tonight? Charles felt no jealousy, after all, she had watched them often enough, but still, he wondered how he would feel actually seeing his wife with another man.

There was more pain from below, and it was pretty obvious Charles would be so fucking turned on watching his wife suck another man's cock, and to see him sliding it inside her married pussy. Charles would love to be underneath as they fucked - licking and lapping up their combined juices as Edward's cock moved in and out of his wife's pussy.

Edward now had one hand on her pussy and the other on her round arse. Slowly and gently he touched both areas but made no attempt to penetrate her. Instead, he rubbed the palm of his hand over her clit, whilst the other hand pushed between her buttocks and Charles could only imagine that he was doing the same with the plug up her arse.

Eleanor groaned a little as she moved in rhythm to his touch, "Mmm, it's no wonder that Charles can't get enough of you Edward."

After a few minutes of rubbing and gyrating, she suddenly broke away from him.

"Now Edward," she continued, "Dress me in my new outfit." She said, stepping out of Edward's reach and opening the cardboard box which was hidden underneath the bed. She took out a shiny thick black double ended dildo and placed it on the bed, and then she took out a latex catsuit, full-length gloves and two pairs of thigh length high heel latex boots of different sizes. She picked up the dildo, squatted down slightly to open her cunt and slid half of it straight in until the mid-section rested against her entrance, then surprisingly reached to her rear and pulled out the butt plug, which she tossed in Charles's direction.

"Edward, help me with this catsuit," She ordered as Charles looked down at the shiny plug which had come to rest near his naked feet. Quickly, he brought his attention back to the scene unfolding in front of him. Edward took the catsuit from the bed and helped Eleanor step into It. He then pulled it up her legs, stopping at her silky thighs to smooth out the lower half of her lubricated legs. He then continued to smooth out and pull up the cat suit to just below her dildo. Eleanor reached down, pushing the dildo through a hole in the front of the suit so Edward could continue to enclose her curved arse in smooth red latex. He took extra care to ensure the latex was pushed between her cheeks not only to extenuate her curves but also to make certain the rear internal sheath was pushed right up her arse.

Eleanor pulled up the front of the suit and slipped into the arms as Edward began to zip up from the base. She wiggled a bit her sexy body to help as he zipped up the back of the suit to the top of the neck to encase her whole body.

"Now… for the finishing touches. Take that silk rag from out of the box and polish my red latex skin," she instructed while pulling on her thigh length boots and enclosing her sexy legs and thighs in the second layer of beautiful plastic.

Edward polished her body, wiping away any traces of the lubrication to reveal a deep glossy shine. When finished, he stood back to admire his excellent work. The tightness of the catsuit erotically extenuated her curves, her big tits pushed together by the cut of the suit and her stiff nipples pushing through the latex. She looked like a silky red goddess ready for fucking with her black rubber cock jutting out in front, twitching in excitement as her hungry, wet cunt contracted around it.

"Looks like my little fuck toy is feeling a little left out," she laughed, "I think we should have him join in the fun. Here Edward, put this on him," she said, handing him the latex make that Charles had last worn the night he'd first met Edward and his wife.

He took the mask from Eleanor and walked up to Charles with a smile on his face. Charles bowed his head forward so he could put it on, but Edward lifted his chin so he could hold eye contact for a couple of seconds. Passionately he kissed Charles on the lips, before pulling the mask over Charles's face. The familiar feeling of excitement returned as his sense of sight was removed and he felt the tightening of the latex on his skin as Edward zipped up the back of the hood.

"Lube up those beautiful smooth legs Edward," Eleanor whispered.

Charles heard Edward rubbing lube into his palms and then waited for him to make contact with him again. "God, that feels so good!" Charles thought as

Edward spread the lube over his hairless legs. Every single stroke seemed to be intensified by the smoothness of the skin, especially as he worked his way up and rubbed between his legs, triggering a slight shudder through his cock which then began to dribble as he imagined it was just inches away from Edward's face.

"Now put these on him."

Charles was now slightly confused as Edward lifted up one of his feet and then realised who the second pair of thigh length latex high heels that Eleanor, had removed out of the box were for, as he slipped Charles foot into the boot. Out of everything they had done recently, Charles was unsure about wearing women's boots. This was something he was just a little uncomfortable about, compared with feeling excited about sucking another man's dick for the first time or Eleanor taking him up the arse with her strap-on. Maybe there was a fine line that Charles was not willing to cross between becoming a submissive fuck toy and becoming a sissy cuck husband.

Edward pulled up the latex boot over Charles's knee and almost to the top of his thigh. It was quite uncomfortable to stand up and balance in and he was still not sure about all of this until he zipped up the back of the boot and he felt the incredible tight sensation of being sheathed in rubber. Edward did not need to take his other foot; Charles carefully balanced on one heel and offered it to him, impatient to experience the same sensual feeling again.

"Wow, you look so fucking sexy in those boots, Charles," Eleanor commented. Without waiting for an answer, Eleanor stood directly in front of him, tracing her fingers down his neck and chest.

"Lube my hole Edward, make it nice and slippery while I suck my husband's cock."

Eleanor pulled her husband's hips towards her and took all of him in her mouth. Charles imagined Edward walking up behind her, his cock hard, throbbing and dripping with pre-cum as he began rubbing lubrication into her hole for the first time. Eleanor bit down on his cock making him flinch in pain and surprise and then pulled away.

"Oh, come on Edward, don't play with it, lube my fucking arse hole. I want three of your fingers inside me," Eleanor reprimanded before returning her attention back to Charles's cock. Edward obeyed, which made Eleanor moan with pleasure as she sucked hungrily whilst rocking back and forth, spit roasted on her husband's cock and Edward's fingers.

She withdrew slightly, "Edward, fuck my tight arse with a dildo - fuck it hard as you masturbate my strap-on." She returned back to Charles cock, taking it deeper as Edward inserted the dildo up her arse hole, the more he thrust the more she was forced onto Charles's cock, he could only imagine the scene in front of him as Edward fucked her arse and played with her rubber cock; the mere thought of it was speeding Charles towards another ejaculation.

Eleanor picked up the pace as Edward thrust more forcibly, she moaned louder in pleasure, then relaxed her lips from Charles's cock, her breath was becoming shorter and shorter, then suddenly her hands moved along the top of the latex boots he was wearing, her nails dug into the flesh at the back of his exposed thighs, pulling him towards her and driving his cock deep down her throat forcing Charles to cum as her own climax shuddered through her.

"Edward, clean him up," She ordered breathlessly, "and then bring him to the bed."

Edward began to greedily suck Charles's cock, maintaining his erection. When done he untied Charles's restraints and guided him towards the bed.

"Now it's Charles's turn to clean me up," Eleanor said, her breathing was returning to normal.

With that, Edward bent Charles over the end of the bed and he felt Eleanor direct him towards her, half expecting to suck on her cock, but instead Charles was met by her warm wet pussy.

"My husband's arse is all yours to tease, Edward, bring him to the edge again while he cleans me."

She forced Charles deeper into her cunt and he began to lick at her juices, while Edward pulled his arse cheeks apart and began to lick around the rubber moulded bristles rubbing the opening of his hole. Charles's cock strained in anticipation and pleasure, and he began to rock backwards and forwards between his wife's cunt and Edward's probing tongue. He could feel her gently gyrating in rhythm, and Edward's warm breath on his arse. His hands then moved up and down his legs and latex boots, up his inner thigh then caressed his constrained smooth balls and shaft, drawing cum from his hard cock.

Charles began to moan in pleasure and as if this was a signal, Eleanor pushed him deeper into her with one hand as the other hand scrapped down the back of his spine, causing him to arch his back, and allowing Edward to probe his arse deeper.

"Give him what he wants Edward," Eleanor said. Then suddenly she pulled the harness at the top of Charles's arse and released the catch. The strap between his cheeks slackened then fell between his legs, exposing his eagerly awaiting smooth arse hole to Edward.

His legs almost gave way in excitement, having imagined this for so long. Edward's fingers lingered at his hole, teasing it open as he pushed and licked his arse. He pushed at his arse muscles, opening his hole slightly to welcome his warm tongue into his entrance whilst Eleanor pushed his face deeper into her; she was getting warmer and wetter.

Edward stopped what he was doing and placed his hands firmly on Charles's waist as he moved himself closer, Eleanor pushed Charles away then slid the double ended dildo back into her wet cunt.

"Charles, Suck and fuck me," she requested, pushing her black cock into his mouth.

Edward positioned his cock at the entrance to Charles's hole, teasing him, knowing that he wanted it so badly. Charles tried to push backwards, but Eleanor held him firmly on her cock, pulling him and making him gag as she plunged herself deeper down his throat.

Edward shuffled closer; the tip of his leaking cock twitched gently at Charles's entrance, exciting and tantalising as he flexed his rear muscles to take him inside. And then simultaneously, Edward thrust forward as Eleanor pushed backwards and Charles was impaled on his cock. He let out a gasp of pain and pleasure as Edward hit his prostrate and squeezed his hips to ensure he was as deep as possible.

"Fuck him hard, Edward... Hard!" Eleanor ordered, pushing her husband's head back, then pulling him closer, thrusting her rubber cock back into his mouth.

Edward did not need to be asked twice, Charles felt him withdraw then lunge back inside in rhythm to his wife's movements. He was in ecstasy, as he slid his big cock in and out. Eleanor was reeling in her own word, forcing her husband deeper onto her cock, which in return was stimulating the dildo inside her.

Charles was so fucking close, wrapped up in experiencing what he had yearned for weeks, Edward's cock firmly inside, along with the added excitement of wearing thigh length latex boots and having his mouth fucked by his wife.

Eleanor's breath became quicker and shorter as she started to climax and in response to Edward's thrusts became stronger and more forceful. Then she orgasmed with an almighty scream, pushing her cock down his throat, Edward's shaft and balls stiffened, and Charles went wild with excitement and anticipation waiting to feel his spunk shoot inside him.

Edward dug his nails into Charles' waist, violently pulling him back onto his erect cock, and Charles could feel the warm spunk filling his tight hole. Edward twitched, sending yet another load deep inside, he thrust his hips forward, banging once again against Charles's prostrate and as he shot the last of it, Charles relaxed, clenching his sphincter muscles around Edward's cock, feeling his cum dribble from his hole. I reached my climax and I came all over the bed and Eleanor's thighs. Quickly she wiped it from her thighs and rubbed it onto her rubber dick before shoving it back in Charles's mouth so that he could taste his own cum on her cock.

Edward withdrew completely from Charles's arsehole, he could feel he was open, his arse stretched as much as it possibly could. He pushed more of his hot sperm from out his arse and Edward instantly began to suck on Charles's cum filled hole.

He groaned in pleasure and let out a large gasp as Edward grabbed hold of his cock and jerked his second load of fresh spunk onto the bed.

Charles had finally become his *hotwife's* bi-sex toy.

Printed in Great Britain
by Amazon

79767566R00059